I0649145

Percy Hemingway

The Happy Wanderer

& other verse

Percy Hemingway

The Happy Wanderer
& other verse

ISBN/EAN: 9783337406448

Printed in Europe, USA, Canada, Australia, Japan

Cover: Foto ©Andreas Hilbeck / pixelio.de

More available books at **www.hansebooks.com**

By the same Author.

OUT OF EGYPT.

STORIES FROM THE THRESHOLD OF THE EAST.

Crown 8vo, 3*s*. 6*d*. net.

THE HAPPY WANDERER.

Of this Edition 500 *copies only have been printed for England and America.*

The Happy Wanderer & other Verse
By Percy Hemingway

LONDON
ELKIN MATHEWS
1896
CHICAGO
WAY & WILLIAMS

CONTENTS.

v

MORE than a dozen of the following poems have appeared in the "Academy," and two have been printed in the "Pall Mall Gazette." For their courtesy in allowing me to reprint them, my thanks are due to the proprietors and editors of both journals.

IN MEMORIAM

RODEN NOEL

(Obiit May 26th, 1894).

ALAS! that even poets die,
    The men who keep the old world young,
Who know God's deepest mystery,
But fall e'er half their song is sung.

Still had the sun, the stars of night,
And waves of haunted Cornish seas,
A million jewels exquisite
Stored for you in their treasuries.

The doors are shut, the locks are sealed,
And many weep above your grave,
Some for the secrets unrevealed,
And all remembering what you gave.

But I, who loved your songs and you,
A gracious presence still shall meet,
On peaceful days of August blue,
Haunting Port Wrinkle's tiny street.

1

Together we'll the footpath take
That wends to high cliff solitudes,
And see the tower of far Landrake
The autumn dyed St. Germans' woods ;

Gaze far across the sea-fed tide,
The Hamoaz' waters glancing bright,
Towards Plymouth, dazzling as a bride
Sun-smitten in her robes of white.

And when Tregantle's brow is won,
And, 'mid the bracken and the grass,
We hear the solemn unison
Of wild bees singing as they pass,

And those great waves of Cornwall roar
Along the coast from Rame to Looe,
The truths of God and earth once more
I know that I shall learn from you.

THE HAPPY WANDERER.

HE is the happy wanderer who goes
    Singing upon his way, with eyes awake
To every scene, with ears alert to take
The sweetness of all sounds, who loves and knows
The secrets of the highway, holds the rose
Is fairer for the wounds the briars make :
He welcomes rain that he his thirst may slake,
The sun because it dries his dripping clothes:

Treasures experience beyond all store,
Careless if pain or pleasure he shall win.
So that his knowledge widen more and more
Ready each hour to worship or to sin,
Until tired, wise, content, he halts before
The sign o' the Grave, a cool and quiet inn.

3

A VOICE FROM THE BUSH.

THE white gums by the moonlight bleached
   Like ivory columns show,
But fairer are the English woods
   Where elms and beeches grow.

The awful silence of the bush
   Weighs heavy on my heart,
But west winds rustle in the trees
   Above the winsome Dart.

Of Marazion, white Penzance,
   Kit Hill and Antony,
I dream o' nights, and pray that God
   Take not my dreams from me.

Beverly,
  West Australia.

4

THE COMING OF THE NIGHT WIND.

THE broad blue sky into purple darkens,
  The sapphire glory of ocean fades,
The panting earth for the night wind hearkens,
The temple pillars cast longer shades.

The hot, strong life of the sun is failing
Whose fiery kisses smote flower and tree,
The white moon over the palms is sailing
A phantom ship on a waveless sea.

The earth is still as a heart whose beating
Is stayed a moment through hope or fear,
But the great stars glow with a golden greeting
And the pilot cross to the south is clear.

Then a sudden flash on a far wave breaking,
A stir as the grasses begin to nod,
And the nervous rustle of palm leaves shaking
Herald the night wind that flies from God.

Colombo.

"Say, pilgrims, art thou for the East indeed?"
BROWNING.

AYE, truly to the golden East I go,
 Leaving these city streets, the fog, the rain.
The restless search for rest that none obtain,
The ceaseless noise, the voices hoarse with woe
For fair things blotted out, for hill and plain
Black-scarred with dismal houses row on row;
Now step I gladly towards the sunrise glow
To find earth's beauty and God's truth again.

There where the wilderness and ocean meet
And clumps of slender palm their shadows fling,
The presence of the Invisible I greet.
His flight is as a seabird's on the wing,
His voice is as the blue sea's murmuring,
His peace the desert's at the noontide heat.

6

To W. Y.

GOD I thank, for I have found
    Health and vigour in this place;
But for this I thank him most,
That he brought us face to face.
Not endowed with scholarship,
Knowing not the world of books,
You have learnt in many a fight
How a foreign foeman looks.
You have heard the bullets whiz,
Charged brave-hearted in the van,
Over Egypt's scorching plains,
Through the wilds of Hindustan.
That is more than scholarship,
Facing death with steady eye,
Only swearing if you fall
Like an English lad to die.
I have learnt 'mid Oxford halls
Books that men have counted wise,
Studied many a sage's words,
Dreamed o'er vain philosophies.
You were wiser far than I
In the way you chose your lot;

Not the man who dreams, my friend,
Is the truest patriot.
Now farewell—and fare you well,
We must yield to fate's decrees,
Egypt's sun will shine o'er you
While I cross dividing seas.
Dover's cliffs are vaunted fair,
Pleasant is our native land,
But my thoughts will often turn
Back to Ramleh's golden sand.
And I'll think of you, my friend,
Every time a health I drain,
Glancing forward to the day
That shall bring you home again.
When you quaff in thoughtful mood
Liquor we have often quaffed,
When across your memory run
Ghosts of jests at which we've laughed,
When the " Paradiso " band
Twangs my favourite melody,
Just this thing I ask of you,
Drink a silent health to me.

Fort Kom-el-dik,
    Alexandria.

OUTWARD BOUND.

SWALLOW strong upon the wing,
  Dying Autumn bids us fly—
Over is the harvesting,
We must hasten, you and I.
Now September's reign is done,
Brown the earth and bare the trees,
Time our exodus begun,
Speed we o'er the Arab seas.

In bazaars I'll stroll again
Rich with gems and woven wares,
See the temples of the plain,
Hear the buzz of eager prayers;
Wander by the lonely lake,
Burnished glass of burnished skies,
Where no winds the waters shake,
Where the wan-faced lotus lies;
Climb the thickly wooded steep,
Mingled scents of spices breathe,
Watch the frothing waters leap
Fiercely to the vale beneath;
'Mid the terraced rice fields glide,
Where the sun-browned Tamil plods,

9

Ranged along the mountain side
Like a staircase of the Gods ;
Wander on the lonely shore
Where the ocean, vast and calm,
Cringes like a slave before
Lordly rows of silent palm ;
Then as sombre shadows steal,
Heralds of the night, o'er all,
Watch the flashing fire-flies wheel
In their mazy carnival.

Swallow strong upon the wing,
Swallow with the foam-stained breast,
Winter clouds are gathering,
Snow is on the mountain crest,
Raindrops patter on the eaves,
Soughs the wind and moans the sea,
But the dream my fancy weaves
Bears me outward-bound with thee.

DISENCHANTMENT.

WELL I remember when that saintly face
    I dare not kiss, too clear it looked and fair,
As if heaven's purity were centred there,
When in her smile God's smile I seemed to trace;
I longed my heart beneath her feet to place,
And as priests humbly on the altar stair
Kneel down to pray, I bent the knee in prayer,
Asking her love as they the Father's grace.

I am no longer suppliant at the shrine,
Granted the prize that promised so to bless;
For all has fled from it that was divine,
I loathe and yet I long for her caress,
Shrinking I bid her kiss these lips of mine;
My happiness lies in unhappiness.

FULFILLED DESIRE.

WHY pity her or visit him with blame?
    She does not need men's pity, Semele,
Accomplished was her life's desire when he,
The royal Zeus, from heaven to wed her came.
With swimming eyes her lover thus to see,
Clasped in his arms to murmur once his name,
To feel his kisses smite her lips like flame,
And then to die; could fortune kinder be?

Life's climax reached, to pass from out men's sight
Is God's most perfect gift; the smouldering fire
Flames not again once spent its warmth and light,
And memory is a bride of whom men tire.
Happy is he who bids the world " good-night "
In the brave moment of fulfilled desire.

LET WHOSO WILL.

To H. W.

LET whoso will call half that is unclean,
  And over man's backslidings sit and brood,
For I have found rich colours in the mud
And hints of beauty in the dreariest scene:
I have scant patience with that sober mood
That from the world impetuous youth would wean;
Rather be bold and learn what all things mean,
Since scratches will but teach us hardihood.

Meagre our knowledge is, howe'er we plod,
It may be we should love what most we hate
Since none have wisdom this side of the sod:
And He who judges is compassionate,
For in my dusty soul I found of late
The indubitable footprints of the God.

LOVE'S SCHOLAR.

To F.

THY heart my gospel is, my holy writ,
  Which I thy willing scholar cherish well,
As learned monk in his secluded cell
O'er some rare manuscript would patient sit
Hour after hour, deciphering bit by bit,
So that, e'er summoned by the vesper bell,
All became clear that was inscrutable,
And great his joy was to have mastered it.

I, thy sworn hermit, having shunned men's sight,
Studied the writings on my priceless scroll,
Mused o'er the letters till I read them right,
Then gathered the rich meaning of the whole,
Day's labour making sweet my dreams by night,
Its secret bringing comfort to my soul.

14

IN VINCULIS.

AH! must I ever on that moment brood,
　　The climax of one sweet and terrible year?
Should I have thought grey eyes so wondrous clear,
Have kissed red lips in such ecstatic mood,
Have slept on warm white breasts: in solitude
Breathed passionate blasphemies God wept to hear,
If I had known that sin was so austere
And so relentless in its war with good?

No respite is there while this life shall last,
Harsh voices mock me, loud, importunate,
Crying " fool, who found sweet vice was gall too late."
Then when aside my weakness I would cast
There glows before my eyes a form so fair,
" Let me repeat my sin," becomes my prayer.

CONVERSION.

To S. A.

AMONG the sages I a sage will stand.
    So said I once, and straightway did rehearse
Strange theories of the reeling universe,
Denying it was fashioned by God's hand.
Subtle the arguments at my command,
My mouth being as a never emptied purse
Whence words clinked coin-like, and I would disburse,
Gladly, my worthless riches through the land.

Then suddenly upon my lips did fall
A silence, choking up my dismal lies ;
Now I, though pardoned, still for pardon call.
And Love the meaning of the change supplies,
Who, saying little, yet has taught me all,
Gazing full at me with his frank blue eyes.

TO JOHN ADDINGTON SYMONDS.

NOW I would thank you for kind words, my friend,
  For such you bade me call you, laying here
A fading wreath to prove my thanks sincere.
I give you verse, because you oft would send
A word of praise and bid me persevere.
Now is your anchor cast, the cruise at end,
And in my sorrow I scarce comprehend
I shall not meet you, as you schemed, this year.

For I spoke gladly, sauntering down the Strand,
Those last brave words the mail had brought from you,
When a harsh voice proclaimed that you were dead;
And on the callous posters, lo! I read
How you had finished a long journey, through
Eternal Rome to the eternal land.

A SONNET OF DISCOVERY.

MYSELF I see in dream-wrought tapestries,
    Steering my barque where unknown oceans roll
Under the unnamed stars, strange ports my goal
As yet unsought of sailors: or my eyes
Gaze on weird countries at the Southern Pole
Resplendent with unravelled mysteries,
But all my passion for adventures dies
When I would tread the labyrinths of my soul.

My soul! that terrible, dim continent
Full of a silence that affrights my ear,
Where tangled growths my trembling steps prevent.
Where poisonous fevers rot the atmosphere,
And shapes, of hideous dangers imminent,
Between the sombre branches foully leer.

FICTION AND FACT.

All love, that tale should in your heart remain,
That once we read! how homeward came a leal
And faithful knight, scarred by the focman's steel
Fighting for her he loved.   She, in disdain,
Turned aside shuddering at each crimson stain,
Forgetting it was gathered for her weal,
And laughed to scorn each piteous appeal.
Tearfully you whispered, " fool, such love were gain."

Aye, you could weep, who have for me no tears,
Only cold scorn and hate, and yet to win
A smile, a kiss, I did your biddings well.
For you I mocked at heaven and dared to sin,
My soul was in your service, and it bears
Stains burnt upon it by the fires of hell.

BY THE NORTHUMBERLAND ARMS.

TARTAREAN blackness! moon and starshine bright
Blurred by a thousand chimneys' murderous fumes :
There a great warehouse through the darkness looms
A hideous, half-seen monster of the night ;
Here a gaunt factory human souls entombs ;
And down the dreary street to left and right
The flickering gaslamps shed a feeble light,
And every alley poisonous stench exhumes.

Noises there are of waggons lumbering on,
Of whips cracked over horses weak and lean,
Children's shrill voices, all their sweetness gone,
Laughter of hungry men, at jests obscene,
Hurled at a woman, drunken, pale and wan,
Striving to earn a kiss with smile unclean.

THE END OF THE VISIT.

SHALL I visit the places I love so and dwelt in this
      summer again,
See the hedge-rows grow white with rose in each Devon-
      shire lane,
And the sun dash a glory of gold on the moor through the
      mist and the rain?
Shall I watch the waves rush round the headland and race
      through the bay,
And the white gulls that circle above them in quest of
      their prey?
Will my heart become sick with a longing to hear the
      winds roar
Over blue waters bursting to foam on the edge of the shore?
For the pulse of the ocean stirs passion and life in my
      breast,
Yet I find in its spirit unrestful the secret of rest.

See, the sun's gone to sleep, shadows gather, the day's very
      old,
And from Brixham the smacks of the fishers, whose sails,
      red and gold
From the glow of the west, the wind stirs in, weigh anchor
      and glide

21

Away to deep seas on the swell of the out-going tide,
See, the moon rises over the pine trees and flashes its light
On a ship steering steadily south through the gloom of the
    night,
And eager are hearts that she carries with envy to roam
In those far away cities and lands where men long for their
    home,
And would willingly barter their palms and their spices
    and gains
For a glimpse of this Devonshire bay, for a stroll in these
    Devonshire lanes.

    Torbay, 1892.

A HEATHER SONG.

'MID the heather, 'mid the heather! we have lain there,
      you and I,
With the waves below us breaking into silver on the shore,
Gleaming clumps of gorse anear us and the gold sun in
      the sky,
And our ears alert to hearken all the secrets of the moor.

'Mid the heather, 'mid the heather! we have lain there
      side by side
Watching gallant ships sail seaward and the lark above us
      soar,
And the wild bees, honey seeking, in the purple caverns
      hide ;
Then God's blessing seemed upon us in the stillness of the
      moor.

Ah the heather, the sweet heather and the the gorse's
      golden glow,
The lark's song, the dreamy silence, and the blissful days
      of yore !
We have laughed together often, but my ship must
      seaward go ;
You will lie and weep alone, dear, in the sunlight on the
      moor.

23

SOUL AND BODY.

ONE old and weak and crooked and thin
   Played softly on his violin,
Such music from its great heart stirred
As God, till then, had never heard.
A youth who heard the violin,
Declared, " It is the soul must win."

For hearkening to the violin,
As garments soiled and worn and thin
He cast his earthly lusts away.
His soul kept spotless holiday,
And ravished by the violin
Seemed heaven itself to enter in.

Then ceased the magic violin ;
One kissed him with red lips of sin,
And drew him to her dwelling place.
So all night long in her embrace
He watched the moonlight enter in
To spy upon them in their sin.

TRAVELLERS.

To J. B. K.

WE shall lodge at the Sign of the Grave, you say :
  Yet the road is a long one we trudge, my friend,
So why should we grieve at the break of the day ?
Let us drink, let us love, let us sing, let us play,
We can keep our sighs for the journey's end.

We shall lodge at the Sign of Grave, you say :
Well, since we are nearing the journey's end,
Our hearts must be merry while yet they may.
Let us drink, let us love, let us sing, let us play,
For perchance it's a comfortless inn, my friend.

Oxford.

THIS SUMMER NIGHT.

To M. W.

THIS summer night the skies are clear,
  And voiceless is the atmosphere,
The leaves hang motionless as lead,
The flowers are rigid as the dead,
There broods o'er earth a nameless fear.

Like fallen planets now appear
The distant lights, that seem so near,
Through far off streets of Plymouth spread,
                    This summer night.

No human voice sounds forth to cheer,
The only stir that greets the ear
Is a faint murmur overhead,
As if God stepped with stealthy tread
Because the hour of doom is near,
                    This summer night.

AT ST. GERMANS.

To H. B.

EVEN as the singing bee
   Fills with honey sweet the hive,
I, in cells of memory,
   Store the hours I'd keep alive.

I shall not forget the mist
   Curling over Dodman head,
Nor the blue and amethyst
   Through eternal ocean spread.

I'll remember every day
   Ships upon their voyagings,
Hiss and glimmer of the spray,
   Whirr and flash of seabird wings.

What the west wind's gentle breath
   Murmured on the day we met,
I shall not forget till Death
   Leads me where no men forget.

27

THE CONSPIRACY.

WE have laid a plot for Sleep
  That he little bargained for,
Lest he to our chamber creep
Cupid watch and ward will keep
Fully armed by yonder door,
    Sweet conspirator.

Were I lonely or in pain
  Then perchance on Sleep I'd cry,
Here I would from dreams refrain,
They with all their joys contain
Naught like this reality
    On thy breast to lie.

IMPRESSION IN CORNWALL.

THE angry sun has struck his tent
  And hastened to the shades below,
His warmth and glory idly spent.
The rocks are piled against the foe
In granite tier and battlement.

The encroaching waves are vast to-night,
O'er leagues of shore their war-cry rings,
The gulls above them in delight
Cry " forward, forward," as their wings
Flash back the wild moon's frenzied light.

Port Wrinkle,
  Cornwall.

GIFTS FOR MY LADY.

MAKE me a ring, O master goldsmith,
   Make me a ring of brightest gold,
Rival the sun, the great god's goldsmith,
My heart to-day has its secret told.

Make me a glorious scarf, O weaver,
Of red and yellow broidery,
Hues goddesses wear at eve, O weaver,
When revels blaze in the western sky.

On her white, white breast she'll wear, O weaver.
The gorgeous scarf, the scarf I bring her,
And the golden ring, O master goldsmith,
Shall circle my lady's dainty finger.

WAITING.

AMONG the hills I had been half content,
  Sharing the peace of God that on them lies,
Where naught could wake me from those memories
Of moments with you spent.

Beside the sea I were half happy too,
Since wave-like you o'erwhelmed me with your love.
And on the flowing tides are gleams that move
Blue as your eyes are blue.

But 'mid the city's hum life is not sweet,
I watch for you until the day is dead,
And hearken all night long to hear your tread
Startle the silent street.

THE PLEASAUNCE OF THE CITY CHILDREN.

HERE in the heart of the grimy town
    Is the fairest spot that the children see,
An acre of grass-plot bare and brown,
Six scanty shrubs and a stunted tree ;
Though sorrier garden scarce could be
To make the heart of the weary gay,
It rings at evening with mirth and glee—
This is the place where the children play.

Round it the dingy terraces frown,
The fog hangs over it ceaselessly,
Never a bud shall the rose bush crown,
Nor daisy lurk in the grass, ah me !
Birds on their voyages o'er it flee,
None for a song's space cares to stay,
Bound for the vastness of moor and lea—
This is the place where the children play.

Never the roar of the streets can drown
Songs that the children shout lustily,
Glad is the crowd of the tattered gown,
Though out at elbow and frayed at knee :
This is the kingdom of faëry,
For work is over at close of day,
Here for one jubilant hour they're free—
This is the place where the children play.

Prince, this ballade I make for thee,
Listen awhile to thing I say,
Thy palace gardens are fair to see—
This is the place where the children play.

THEOLOGY.

GOD loves me, dear, I know so well,
  Because I stand as sentinel
On every road love passes by;
Because when at love's side I lie
Not God himself my bliss can tell;

Because I sang, when evening fell,
A hymn that, turning vilanelle,
Would prattle of a sea-blue eye—
    God loves me, dear.

Because I only wish to dwell
A captive in love's subtle spell,
And this is my theology.
" To love I pray, for love I'd die
Despising heaven and daring hell "—
    God loves me, dear.

DESERT SICK.

AH me, my heart is sad to-day
  For a sight of the palm clumps far away
On the golden sand of Aboukir bay.

I am sick of the long, gray, gaslit street,
And the tiresome tramping of jaded feet,
For the Arab footsteps are dumb and fleet.

The Thames, fog-ridden, is full of care
For the grim, great barges that float on her,
But the dahcybeahs move light as air.

Here all is noise, though never a tune,
But the Nile winds softly 'neath sun and moon
To the supple song that the rushes croon.

Here skies are dun, and there amethyst ;
In the desert Silence and God keep tryst,
And nothing stirs lest a word be missed.

1894.

THE old year dies! I bury memories,
   Some o'er whose grave I shall not linger long,
Others whose ghosts will always round me throng,
Crooning the echoes of old reveries.
Night, on your dusky breast a tyrant dies,
Who struck a discord in my life's full song,
Laughed at my weakness when he did me wrong,
Then bribed my grief with jewelled ecstasies.

Now, lo! The new year comes with lance in rest,
To seize his father's throne, to rule his thralls,
Eager alike to curse or make us blest,
Scourging or crowning as his humour calls;
The tired old world is murmuring oppressed,
While from the peaceful stars a promise falls.

THE TYRANT.

LOVE'S tyranny now wherefore should I praise,
   Not being enamoured of my altered plight!
I often sigh, who once sang roundelays,
I know the sleepless gnomes that haunt the night.

I burn with feverish jealousy to hear
Words that were spoken when I was not near,

I shroud my eyes from sights I dare not see,
Yet whoso spies must tell his tale to me.

Madman am I, who give my vote for death,
Yet heed not the grim hand that beckoneth.

Love I entreat to go, and while I pray
Grasp him with nervous fingers lest he stray.

Ah, than love's blessing is no deadlier curse,
And yet—and yet—to live undamned were worse.

THE REFUGEE.

IT is my fate to suffer, this I know,
　For I have touched the stinging hand of Sin,
And where he beckoned jauntily would go,
Learnt all his tricks and skilful grew therein.

Then love for you sprung in me unaware,
And love of me made you my perils share ;

So in the midnight hour I lie aghast
Watching fell dreams begotten of the past ;

And yet I know were life again begun
Each deed should be redone that has been done.

That there's no scourge for you should please me well
If I dared face the loneliness of hell ;

But in love's blazing aureole I must hide,
And slink to heaven, unnoticed, at your side.

IN TORBAY.

THE moon has touched the midmost heaven and all the
    stars grow pale,
The furthest ridge of shore is reached on which the wave-
    lets break,
'Tis time to weigh the anchor now, 'tis time to hoist the
    sail
If we'd float away on the ebb, my boys, or ever the world's
    awake.

We'll steer our vessel eastward ho to greet the coming day,
And chase the shadows flying over leagues of purple sea :
How bravely on our faces will the fresh salt breezes play,
As we speed on our course o'er the heaving deep to see
    what the dawn shall be.

Amid the bonny mackerel that around us gleam and leap.
Rocked on the rollers lazily, throughout the day we'll lie ;
And make for port and home again when all the world's
    asleep
By the light of the new-born moon and stars aloft in the
    quiet sky.

LOVERS.

LOVE the Protector said, "I know the man,
He is my friend, abuse him as you will,
His vices were an easy thing to scan,
But I can weigh his virtues by my skill."

Love the Protector, frowning, further said,
"From my embrace no good is banished."

Love the Protected, sighed on bended knee,
"In my soul's lord no evil can I see,

"For in his presence I may doff the sham,
Because he loves me even as I am."

Such is the love of friends in every land,
But only they who love may understand;

Yet should the mockers stint the scornful nod
Remembering the loves of men and God.

WERE I SULTÂN.

WERE I Sultân, then every land
    Should be a plaything in my hand,
The bastions of my enemies
Should totter underneath their cries
When flashed my sword in Samarcand.

And noble youths should form a band
Of warriors keen for my command,
Swifter their charge than eagle flies,
              Were I Sultân.

I'd laugh to hear the suppliant's sighs;
Yet, if I garnered from your eyes
A wish to humble me, The Grand,
Before you as a slave I'd stand
And cease to carve men destinies,
              Were I Sultân.

IN VENICE.

FROM each canal songs loiter on the air,
    The stars and kindly moon
      Search the lagoon
Finding sweet portraits there.

But not for me is beauty in the place.
    The wavelets as they fall
      Thy voice recall,
The flickering lights thy face.

ALL SOULS' NIGHT.

THIS All Souls' night, to solace my desire,
   The board with meats and heartening wines is spread,
For I, in joyful terror, by the fire
Would see some shadowy lover leave the dead.

Lo, I would gather from his noiseless breath
The wisdom stored the further side of Death,

While the mysterious, wistful, midnight gloom
Should palpitate with passions of the tomb.

But 'tis no phantom wooes me on this night;
My lover's limbs are strong, his heart is light,

He thinks with lusty songs to please my ear,
He dreams that burning kisses scorch the tear,

Nor does he guess I cheat my eyes to see
The ghost of what I once thought love would be.

43

UNDER THE OLIVE TREES.

LO where the silent olives make
　　Dim clouds of green on yonder hill,
Dear heart, dear heart, for love's sweet sake
The stealthy midnight lingers still.

Love flees the sun's impetuous fire,
The curious gaze of moon and star,
Because the Land of Heart's Desire
Is where the sombre shadows are.

Corfu, 1894.

SONG OF THE YOUNG SAILOR.

I'M weary of the rolling waves, the tempest and the rain,
And I would that now in Plymouth Sound our good ship
rode again,
'T were sweet to sight the Eddystone, to round the Rame
once more,
To lie at anchor 'neath the shade of Edgecumbe's wooded
shore ;
For Plymouth is the fairest town that stands beside the sea,
Ten years of life I'd gladly give in Plymouth town to be.

I have a friend in Plymouth town, and search through ev'ry
land
You will not find a warmer heart nor clasp a trustier hand,
And every time he thinks upon his comrade on the sea
He heaves a sigh, and drains a glass, and breathes a prayer
for me ;
O God, to have one hour again of those glad hours we
knew !
Old friend, I long to clink a glass and smoke a pipe with you.

In Plymouth town a maiden lives, beside the Barbican,
And truer woman never yet was wife to mortal man,
Her prayers go far beyond the stars, though they are far
away,
For God and angels silent are when she kneels down to pray ;
O would I were in Plymouth town, my heart and soul at
rest,
To kiss again those lips of hers, to sleep upon her breast.

King George's Sound,
West Australia.

45

FINIS.

NO more we'll wander where the wood is deep,
    Searching the silence at the heart of June ;
No more on yonder hill be lulled to sleep
By drowsy scent of bracken at mid-noon :
Now we must feign that in each other's face
The passionate kisses have not left their trace ;
And only echo, of old words we said,
The sword-sharp, lying sentence, " love is dead."

Bravely we'd greet the ills that lie before
If what made glad the past were surely o'er,
But Love, being outraged, moulds a sterner fate,
He binds us while he bids us separate,
So half our years loom grim before us yet
To brood upon the days we must forget.

  Corfu.

QUATRAINS.

TO

F. YORK POWELL,

THESE QUATRAINS.

THE SEA.

THOUGH lute or viol make sweet melody
    When o'er them lovingly deft fingers stray,
The noblest music thunders from the sea,
That mighty organ only God can play.

EROS AND PSYCHE.

L OVE did not leave his bride long desolate,
    But hastened back to kiss away her pain ;
And yet man's soul knows no such happy fate,
Whose joys once fled will not return again.

A CONTRAST.

MAN places woman on a pedestal,
  And love breeds loathing should the goddess fall;
When man by woman worshipped slips, not so,
Her love increases, weeping for his woe.

A STREET THOUGHT.

WHAT if there be an end of primrose blooms,
  And factories frown where roses had their birth?
Despite the clang of iron and whirr of looms
There is a sound of singing on the earth.

53

PARADOX.

'TIS brave to sail the ocean wastes along
    And greet God there, fierce, mutable and strong :
'Tis sweet to lie beneath the desert palm
And know him still immutable and calm.

FEAR OF DEATH.

THOUGH weary labourers for rest are fain,
  The oldest tremble when they graveward peep;
How should they ever dream of youth again
In that cold chamber where the dead men sleep?

INGRATITUDE.

WHAT fairer thing than youth may men behold,
  Fluting sweet songs and clothed in eastern gold
The poet gives the world eternal youth,
It is the world that makes the poet old.

A NEW VOLUME.

NAY, sweetheart, ask not in my past to look,
  Not yours, and so not mine, its love and spite :
My life to-day is an unlettered book,
And on the empty pages you must write.

IN THE GULF OF CORINTH.

THE perfect artist made all arts his own,
　　Painted the hues o'er yonder sunset thrown,
Carved with firm hand those everlasting hills,
And struck all chords from ocean's monotone.

58

AN APOLOGY.

SINCE I have loved the woods, the stars of night,
  The purple plains, the hills, the sea, the sun,
Discovering truths and mysteries exquisite,
God will not oust me from his benizon.

OF GREAT POWERS.

WHY prate of mighty nations? They are naught.
  Busy with pride or keen for temporal greed;
The individual in each age has fought
And lashed his kind to do the vital deed.

TO A PATIENT LADY.

THOU art not jealous, sweetheart Death, I think,
    Because awhile I shun thy trysting place,
For when upon our marriage couch we sink
There's no one shall disturb our long embrace.

REAL AND IDEAL.

WHEN life before you stands undraped and real,
    Life with her glorious eyes and arms outspread.
Why shun her kiss to woo some dim ideal
Framed in the future, dust among the dead?

IN LOVE'S GARDEN.

I AM your garden, since you love me so,
  My thoughts, dreams, even sins, you cull them all ;
Your eyes are as the summer sun, and lo !
My heart the peach that ripens on the wall.

HEREAFTER.

To G. W.

IT may be we shall know in the hereafter
   Why we, begetting hopes, give birth to fears,
And why the world's too beautiful for laughter,
      Too gross for tears.

OFF MISSALONGHI.

MOTHER of memories, of song, of art,
    Not by your victories are you deified ;
I worship you, because a Northern heart
As sacred holds the spot where Byron died.

OFF CAPE MATAPAN.

BLUE cliffs of Greece, and each a sacred spot,
  While Athens calls o'er waves that mock the sun ;
Were I a poet songs were here begot
Whose birth would solace when the voyage was done.

A GRADUATE.

SINCE I have graduated in love's school
   There is not any wisdom left in me—
The man who loves you not I deem a fool,
But whoso loves you is my enemy.

LOVE'S ARROGANCE.

BECAUSE I worship, the wide world must trace
  The glory of a goddess in your face ;
Because I love, you must not dare to give
Another share in my prerogative.

THE SILENCE OF THE WISE.

AND what is love? Such questioning is vain,
Since only they who love not dare explain,
While they that love through jealousy are mute
Lest others rob them of their joy and pain.

THE POET.

How surely unrecorded victories die
    Without example noble acts were few ;
Therefore a poet sometimes passes by
And stirs men to the deeds they dream they do.

"THE ETERNAL FUTURE."

WHAT though at times our laughter break to tears,
And discords mar the song the lover hears,
God gives us one irrevocable gift—
The power of looking forward through the years.

LIFE.

HE only lives who covets life's extremes,
 Snatching a share of kisses and of scars,
Who builds from crumbling hope diviner dreams
And treads in hell the threshold of the stars.

TO SLEEP.

To M. R.

O FLUTTERING sleep, so fearful to alight,
  Poising above me in thy tremulous flight,
Make of my eyes thy chosen branch to-night.

TO "ANTONY."

THERE are recollections float
  Through my brain when nights are still,
Of two fishers in their boat,
Of two huntsmen on the hill;

Of the cricket in the vale
And the tennis at the hall,
Schoolhouse jest and college tale,
Quarrels philosophical;

Of the hours when, side by side,
Laboured we at work and play,
Sought the copse where blackberries hide,
Dreamed the noontide hours away;

Of those evenings when the snow
Fell, and the sou'wester blew,
Sitting in the firelight glow
Plans for coming years we drew;

74

Vowed to work the world some good.
Gain some glory for our names,
Swearing sacred brotherhood
In our sorrows, toils and games.

But the God who shapes our ends
Heeded not our schemes and prayers,
Yet that He has made us friends
Makes us faithful worshippers.

Still to us doth wealth belong,
Memories stirring heart and limb,
Choruses of jovial song,
Echoes of an evening hymn.

Antony Vicarage,
    Cornwall, 1895.

CHISWICK PRESS :—CHARLES WHITTINGHAM AND CO.
TOOKS COURT, CHANCERY LANE, LONDON.

www.ingramcontent.com/pod-product-compliance
Lightning Source LLC
Chambersburg PA
CBHW020047030726
47499CB00007B/2622